Faerytale

Rachael Fuller

Safkhet
Publishing

Safkhet Publishing, Cambridge, United Kingdom

first published by Safkhet Publishing in 2011

1 3 5 7 9 10 8 6 4 2

ISBN 978-1-908208-04-0

A CIP catalogue record for this book is available from the British Library.

Printed and bound by
Lightning Source International

Typeset in 11 pt Franklin Gothic

The colophon of Safkhet is a representation of the ancient Egyptian goddess of
wisdom and knowledge, who is credited with inventing writing.
Safkhet Publishing is named after her because the founders met in Egypt.

Denziens of the Land:

Storyteller	Rachael Fuller
Cover Artist	Carl Stuart-MacRae
Editor	William Banks Sutton
Illustrator	Kim Maya
Proofreader	Will Macmillan Jones

Dedication

For my mother Rosalind and grandmother Eleanor.

All my love always.

Supporting Spirits

You who believe in dreams coming true. You who are there, in the darkness, helping bring the light and make fantasies a reality. You who helped us with your faith in the unseen and fantastical. We honor you here and thank you for all your support.

Charlotte Bell
Anne Cooper
Emily Forsyth
Gerald Harvard
Steve Rogers
Sandra Vaughan

Prologue

Once upon a time, as all good stories start,
There was a little girl who longed with all her heart
To fill her world with magic, and live through stories told,
To wear those ruby slippers, to never dare grow old.

Her Never-Land she found in books: oh, how she longed to go!
But wardrobes failed to lead her to that magic land of snow.
Every thrilling tale she read, the lands they took her to,
The looking glass within her mind would let her journey through.

The other children called her names and wouldn't let her play,
They thought her strange and far too shy, so always kept away.
But she cared not, this little girl, for in the books she read,
Lived many friends from magic worlds, alive within her head.

How she longed to live within the pages of her books,
To challenge evil witches and take back what they took,
Swim in silver seas with mermaids, listen to fairies sing,
And soar across the golden skies, on unicorns with wings.

For life was dull and boring, unlike the books she read,
Where tales of dark enchantment would fill her dreamy head.
Maidens locked in towers, with dragons breathing fire,
While princes fought to save them with arms that never tired.

But little girls who dream too much find wishes do come true,
And in this world this little girl would make her journey through.
For fairy tales, like magic apples, first seem good and sweet,
But one small bite would soon reveal some treats you shouldn't eat!

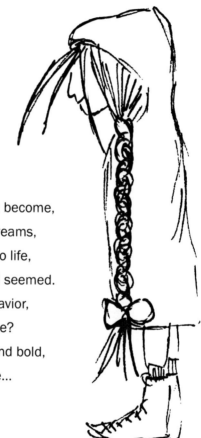

Lost this girl would soon become,
   deep in her land of dreams,
Fairytales now brought to life,
   far darker than they'd seemed.
And who would be her savior,
   who would set her free?
Her older sister, brave and bold,
   she would prove to be...

Ready or not here I come!

"Ready or not, here I come!" little Lucy said,
Then opened up her bright blue eyes that blinked with spots of red.
Through the trees she wildly searched, whilst rooted to the ground,
Somewhere near her sister hid, waiting to be found.

Lucy sighed and stamped her foot, already bored was she,
She loved to hide but not to seek, and why was plain to see.
Her hiding skills were hard to beat, this she knew for sure.
She'd never lost a game you see, not even once before.

A thought came to her in a flash, and with a cheeky grin,
"Are you ready?" she called out, certain she would win.
"Yes!" there came a prompt reply, out from behind a tree,
Then out she came, her sister Ellie, angry as can be.

With bright red cheeks and dirty hair, tied up in bun,
"Dirty cheat" she spat at Lucy, "doesn't mean you've won!"
"Oh yes it does!" Lucy said, her hands upon her hips.
So Ellie stamped her foot again, stuck out her bottom lip.

"Ok! Ok! We'll play again," Lucy quickly said,
And turned around to face the tree, her cheeks becoming red.
She'd won that game fair and square, it really was unjust,
But childish though her sister was, play-along she must.

In every game they played, it's true; it always went the same,
Her little sister got upset and on her laid the blame.
Ellie loved her fairy tales, believed them to be true;
And vowed she always would believe, no matter how she grew.

Lucy teased the dreamy girl and called her silly names,
The childish tales her sister loved, she thought them rather lame!
So when they played their little games, based on stories told,
Lucy moaned and whined throughout, for she was far too old!

Tales of royal beauties, spoilt victims one and all,
Waiting for some pimply prince to take them to a ball.
Trapped in towers, kept as slaves or in an endless sleep,
Fooled by witches, wolves and trolls and far too prone to weep.

Dragons, slain by stuck-up princes, always in the way,
Fairy godmothers casting spells which never last the day.
"Scary" villains pose a threat, evil through and through;
But in the end they always lose no matter what they do.

Lucy was, let it be known, far too old for this.
A frog would still remain a frog, after love's first kiss.
'Forever after' was a lie, as told to little girls,
Who went to bed clutching dolls, with hair tied into curls.

If magic truly did exist then why did grown-ups moan?
Go to work in boring suits and shout down tiny phones.
The world, in truth, was dull and bleak, no fairies to be seen.
Or unicorns to be found, in fields of vivid green.

Ellie did not like it when her older sister teased,
Called her "little fool," and with herself looked pleased.
For she recalled a time before, and not so long ago,
When Lucy's scorn for magic tales wasn't always so.

In the garden Lucy searched, with a stick to poke,
Ellie knew the reason why, to find the "Fairy folk".
Fairies left them coins for teeth and Lucy knew just why:
Children's teeth were used to build their castles in the sky.

"But why use teeth?" Ellie asked, rubbing her cold hands,
"'Cos, children's teeth" said Lucy, "are the whitest in the land!"
She believed their tiny homes would fall down from the sky,
When the fairy living there had reached their time to die.

Ellie mourned for Lucy's loss; in truth she thought it sad,
To lose a world of magic must really feel quite bad.
So she looked all on her own, and bore her sisters scorn,
For glad she was that she could keep her lovely unicorns.

"10, 20, 30, 50!" Lucy called out loud,
Then spun around her face upturned, and shouted to the clouds:
"Ready or not, little fool, once more here I come!
But if you lose and make a fuss, I swear I'm telling mum!"

Then she looked behind the bush where Ellie hid before,
Kicked at mounds of golden leaves upon the forest floor,
Went behind every trunk and up amongst the trees.
She even looked in rabbit holes, and knelt on grubby knees.

Bored she grew, and quickly too, so tried her luck again,
"Are you ready?" she called out as it began to rain.
But no reply did she receive, no laugh nor snap of twig,
When all alone this pleasant forest really seemed quite big!

Rain fell down upon the trees and hung like silver beads.
Then dropped down and turned to mud, mixed up with golden leaves.
The trees they leaned with twisted branches, flexed like giant claws;
Like a mouse, Lucy dodged around their cat-like paws.

She called her sister's name out loud and begged her to come out,
Panic gripped her from within along with seeds of doubt.
Had sulky Ellie stormed off home and left her in the rain?
Or had she gone too far to hide, was stuck somewhere in pain?

Lucy nearly gave up hope, her stomach cramped with dread,
When she saw, through the trees, her sister's coat of red.
All scrunched up, caked with mud, discarded on the floor;
Ellie's coat, there was no doubt, the one she always wore.

It lay beside a rabbit-hole, a large hole it was too,
Large enough for a little girl to crawl the whole way through.
Lucy called her sister's name into the endless black;
She heard it echo through the hole, but no voice answered back.

What if Ellie really thought the game was still in play?
And if she answered that would surely give herself away?
"Little fool!" Lucy said, "She gave me such a fright!"
Then crawled inside the hole herself, though it was very tight.

The hole grew tighter as she crawled; her clothes began to spoil,
Roots hung down around her head, worms wriggled in the soil.
But on she went until she saw a spot of light ahead,
Ellie must have climbed right through and wondered where it led.

Lucy crawled right to the end, so sure of what she would find,

The same old woodland, dull and wet, the one she'd left behind.

There, she'd find her sister, a smug look on her face,

Boasting how she'd found herself the greatest hiding place!

This land so strange and new...

The light it hurt her eyes so much, she tried to keep them closed,
A sickly smell of burning sugar wafted up her nose.
She blindly crawled out of the hole and gasped at what she felt,
The ground beneath was soft and sticky, spongy where she knelt.

As her eyes slowly opened, such a sight she bore,
Sticky grass like candy floss filled the forest floor.
Stranger still the trees bore feathers, peacock ones at that,
A hundred eyes were watching Lucy, nervous where she sat.

Bubbles fell like soft raindrops and pinged upon her nose,
The path beneath was made from glass, cold beneath her toes.
No normal path was this you see, for under glass so bright,
Flowers of every color known were packed in close and tight.

17

Lucy knew not where to look, this land so strange and new,
Another world, far from home she'd followed Ellie to.
"Ellie!" Lucy loudly for her sister called,
Her clothes filthy from the hole through which she'd crawled.

She brushed away the sticky grass, and stood on spongy ground,
Then hopped across with just a step on to the path she found.
The cracks upon the path spread out like tiny silver veins.
It held her weight, creaking, cracking, groaning from the strain.

"Ellie?" Lucy shouted out as loudly as she dared,
Trees shook as though disturbed from their heavy cares.
"Come out now, I've had enough, this game is truly done!
It's getting late we must go home. Come on, you've had your fun!"

No voice called back, nor nervous laugh, confirming Lucy's fear.
The forest groaned its meek reply: Ellie was not here.
Lucy felt the tears well up, whatever would she do?
"I want my mum..." she whimpered, as the tears came through.

Then clenched her fists, grit her teeth and rubbed away the tears,
"Enough!" she said, "Don't be silly! There is no need to fear.
Ellie's here somewhere, I know, I just need to look."
They would leave together, surely, however long it took!

Then from above she heard a sound that made her jump in fright,
A child laughing up above, giddy with delight.
Looking up Lucy gasped, for right up in the tree
There was a girl upon a branch, smiling back in glee.

Staring down with huge great eyes of swampy forest green,
The little girl, or was she so? The strangest she had seen.
"Who are you?" Lucy asked determined to be brave,
The little girl cocked her head then gave a cheeky wave.

As if she weighed no more than air, the strange girl floated down,
Lucy took a big step back, her face creased in a frown.
With pointy ears and spider webs tangled in her hair,
A dress of bracken, moss and leaves, Lucy couldn't help but stare!

"Who are you?" she asked again, feeling less afraid,
"I'm me!" replied the little girl, enjoying the game they played.
Lucy sighed and rolled her eyes. "But what's your name?" she said,
"I'm Zephyr" the girl replied, gracefully bowing her head.

Fluttering in the sun's bright rays, humming with magic's ring,
Upon her back there appeared to be a beautiful pair of wings.
They shimmered like a spider's web and held her up with ease
As if she was a graceful feather, floating on the breeze.

"Are you a...fairy?" Lucy cried, her eyes grew bright and round,
Zephyr wrinkled up her nose and spat upon the ground.
"Yuck!" she cried, "How very rude to think I'm such a thing!
I'm a woodland nymph of course. But...do YOU not have wings?"

Lucy laughed and shook her head, "Wings? I don't have those!"
Zephyr grabbed her arm and sniffed, pulling at her clothes.
"Are you still budding?" Zephyr asked and, turning Lucy round,
With bony fingers Zephyr probed, her feet upon the ground.

As Zephyr poked poor Lucy's back her skin grew red and bruised,
Til Lucy cried, "I'm just a girl!" feeling quite abused.
Jumping back, Zephyr screamed, frantic with despair,
"Just a girl?" she gasped in fear, pulling at her hair.

"You can't be here!" she cried at Lucy, really quite distressed,
"Shoo! Go home, you don't belong! You have to leave!" she pressed.
"I want my sister!" Lucy said, holding back the tears,
"Just tell me have you seen her? Did she come through here?"

"There is another?" Zephyr said, "Tell me it's not so!
Why are you here? What do you want? Please, you both must go!"
"Where is Ellie?" Lucy said, as she'd asked before.
"She came through here, just from that hole, like some magic door."

"Another one?" Zephyr asked, "And is she just like you?
With tiny eyes and grubby knees. Oh, is she wingless too?"
Lucy felt her temper flare, "Oh for goodness sake!"
How she hoped this was a dream, from which she'd swiftly wake.

"Oooh I know!" Zephyr said, no longer struck with fear,
Her panic gone and shocked dismay had all now disappeared.
"Follow me, wingless thing; I know where you should go,
She will tell you what to do; she is bound to know!"

Grabbing Lucy's hand she laughed, "Who would have no wings?
Made to walk on dirty paths upon those five-toed things!"
Lucy frowned but bit her tongue and let her lead the way,
And to herself she softly said, "This is the strangest day!"

Never trust a fairy's tale ...

Lucy's tummy, for want of food,
grumbled in complaint,
Zephyr screamed and jumped in fright,
growing rather faint.
"There's a beast in there!" she cried,
her face turning white,
"Why yes there is," Lucy teased,
"don't get too close, he'll bite!"

Zephyr gasped, eyes wide with fear, her pale cheeks turning red,
"Don't be scared," Lucy said, "he sleeps once he's been fed."
Zephyr flew, quick as a flash, fluttering through the trees,
When in a second, she returned, her hands were full with leaves.

"I'm not eating those!" said Lucy, reeling in disgust,
The leaves were thin and paper dry, the color of golden rust.
Zephyr stuffed her open mouth full of the leaves so dry
With bulging cheeks she offered a leaf, willing her to try.

"They're good!" she mumbled, mouth still full, spitting golden dust,
Though still unsure Lucy said, "I'll try them if I must."
She took the leaf from Zephyr's hand; it shone like dirty gold.
Lucy sniffed the leaf and scowled as though it smelt of mold.

She slowly raised it to her lips, and nibbled on the leaf,
With eyebrows raised her eyes grew wide, and shone with disbelief.
Reaching out, she got some more and crammed her mouth up tight
The leaves dissolved like sugar, scrumptious, sweet and light.

Zephyr laughed and clapped her hands, "Told you so!" she said.
"He won't want me for lunch, now that he's been fed!"
Lucy laughed and licked her lips, brushing at her clothes,
Zephyr babbled on beside her, dancing on tiptoes.

Lucy looked up with delight as she became aware,
The trees above with feathered leaves each held tiny pears!
No normal pears were these, each opened with a door
Inside were tiny tables, and leaves upon the floor.

"What are they?" she asked aloud and reached to pluck one free.
Zephyr slapped her hand away as the pear fell from the tree.
An angry cry came from inside as it hit the ground and split,
Out flew a tiny winged person, shaking its fists in a fit.

"A fairy!" Lucy cried with joy, and reached out in delight,
The fairy flew onto her palm, not fearful of her height.
She raised her hand up to her face, the fairy on tiptoes,
Then cried in pain as the wicked fairy bit her on the nose!

Zephyr laughed and clapped her hands, drifting on her wings,
"That'll teach you!" she laughed with glee and then began to sing:
"Never trust a fairy's tale, for fairies just tell lies...
And never cross a fairy if you value both your eyes!"

Before this darkness grows

Lucy nursed her throbbing nose,
  ignoring Zephyr's voice,
She had to follow this strange nymph;
  she had no other choice.
Who'd have thought that fairies were
  so mean and filled with spite,
When all this time they'd been portrayed
  as all sweetness and delight?

Upon the path they made their way, the trees began to thin,
They reached a lake with secrets far below the water's skin.
'Round about in murky deep, a dirty shade of green,
Swam many tiny mermaids; so small as barely seen.

Lucy knelt by the edge of the lake and leaned out over the side,
The mermaids swiftly scattered, trying their best to hide.
Like wingless fairies did they look, with tails of sapphire blue,
And flowing hair that caught in the light, giving a silvery hue.

By the bank was a shabby hut, old and falling apart,
The door on which they knocked crashed down with a start.
Inside seemed empty, layered with dust, just chairs and a bed,
Cobwebs covered the beams above, much like gossamer thread.

Windows thick with dust and grime, the sun could not shine through,
Upon the glass were plastic sheets, where fairies stuck like glue.
Lucy let out a pitying sigh, then remembered her nose, still sore,
And into the hut she slowly trod, stepping just over the door.

"There's no one here!" Lucy said, as dust flew up her nose,
Then further in, there came a sound from under a pile of clothes.
The mountain moved and turned its head, as dust flew out in clouds,
And from the folds of cloth there came a cackling sound, so loud.

The mountain was a very old woman, her legs like the root of a tree,
Which when planted on the floor below, twisted right up to her knee.
Her skin was thin and dry like bark, her hair matted and wild,
A pair of eyes glinted beneath, and lower, the hint of a smile.

"Come closer you," the woman rasped with a voice like leaves so dry,

"You've nothing to fear from me," she said, as Lucy grew quite shy.

"What a mess I see you're in, so far from home you appear,

I take it you don't wish to stay, for you're not welcome here."

"Your little sister must be found, you both do not belong,

Her strength of mind brought her here; you see that this is wrong.

Our world should not be mixed with yours, in truth they will collide,

Realities will bleed together, the ground will open wide."

"To leave this place you must be brave and face the road ahead,

Much darker horrors you will find than from the books you've read.

For here the tales are not confined to pages safe within,

'Ever-afters' don't prevail; the good don't always win"

Lucy gasped to hear such things, really quite distressed.
"What must I do," she plainly asked "to get me from this mess?"
Outside the skies were starting to change, through the windowpane,
Fading from blue to powdery pink, the bubbles turning to rain.

"Journey through this land you must, until you reach the end,
Then make your jump, both of you, and to your world descend.
But make haste, for time runs out, and darkness smothers the sun,
Shadows invite the Evil Ones; our world will be overrun."

"Your little sister must be found and find her quick you must,
This is her world, or so she thinks, a world in which she trusts.
You will know the path she'd take, which way she'd choose to go
So find her soon, poor little girl, before this darkness grows."

"Take the path and you will pass
  three tales upon your way,
Act as you will but mindful of time,
  for many will delay.
Not all in this land are as pleasant as I,
  and many won't wish you well,
Be on your guard, trust just yourself
  and fall not for any dark spell."

Lucy nodded and walked to the door,
  then turned to say goodbye,
But she was gone; a mound of clothes
  covering glinting eyes.
Outside, Zephyr said goodbye,
  and gave her a dagger of bone.
An enchanted gift, pretty and light,
  so sharp it could cut through stone.

Her huge eyes filled with shiny tears
and, hovering on tiptoes,
"Goodbye little being," she said with a sigh
and kissed her upon the nose.
"I wish I could keep you," she added so softly
that Lucy barely could hear,
Then fluttered away without looking back,
singing through her tears.

Rapunzel, Rapunzel!

Lucy stood by the lake, her head turned to and fro,
"You will know the path she'd take, which way she'd choose to go."
She closed her eyes and heard these words, what would Ellie do?
So thrilling she would find this world, she'd want to journey through.

No trail of breadcrumbs did she leave, if through the woods she went
To find a house of gingerbread or witch to catch her scent.
"Never stray from the path" Red Riding Hood was told,
But stray she did, and poor Grandma's fate would soon unfold.

A road of yellow brick did lie before sweet Dorothy Gale,
She found her way upon that path, along that golden trail.
Lucy jumped upon the path as Ellie would have done,
If she walked fast, she'd find her soon, and spoil Ellie's fun.

Walking along the winding path Lucy raised her head,
A deep pink blush now stained the skies, bleeding into red.
The bubbles turned to soft raindrops; they fell and kissed her face.
Dry as a bone, they smelled like rust and left a bitter taste.

She walked for hours, or so it seemed, over the path of flowers,
Until she reached a clearing where there stood a huge white tower.
It disappeared into the clouds, which smothered the stones so white;
No windows or doors, just a tower of stone – a truly unusual sight.

Beneath a tree there was a man, sobbing in his grief.
Dainty hands covered his eyes, clutching a handkerchief.
"Whatever's the matter?" Lucy asked, saddened by his cries.
"The witch came," he sobbed in grief, "and caught me by surprise!"

"I came to save the lady fair, imprisoned in the tower,
I'm her prince, her sweetest love; she's my precious flower.
But the witch she knew I'd come, and cast her spell on me:
The fairies came and took my eyes – now I cannot see!"

Lucy looked up to the tower, hidden past the clouds,
"It cannot be? But then, who else?" these thoughts she spoke aloud.
This tower she had seen before, but not with her own eyes,
It belonged within her books, with other made-up lies.

She cupped her hands around her mouth and, swallowing her pride,
Called out the words she knew so well, told next to her bedside.
"Rapunzel, Rapunzel, let down your hair!"
   her voice bounced off the stone.
Then from beyond the clouds she heard a disagreeable moan.

The prince he howled, fresh salty tears fell down upon his face.
"Nasty girl!" Lucy said, "and the prince: a waste of space!"
But like it or not Lucy knew just how this tale must end,
Rapunzel must release her hair; her "prince" could then ascend"

Rapunzel, Rapunzel, let down your hair! I'll come and set you free,
The prince has lost his eyes for you; now he cannot see!
Yet he still waits alone and blind, pining for you here,
Please don't be so mean and rude; he really loves you dear."

Soon there came down from above, flying through the air,
Tied up with a satin bow, a plaid of thick blond hair.
It hit the ground, swayed to and fro, then settled in a line,
Grabbing the hair she gave it a tug and found it'd hold her fine.

Gripping it tight she started to climb, feet braced upon the stone,
With every tug, from high up above, there came a feeble moan.
Higher she climbed into the clouds; the prince grew small below,
Until she found she could not hear his shameful cries of woe.

On she climbed not looking down, as her arms began to tire,
Her face all red and wet with sweat, she couldn't go much higher!
"About time!" there came a voice that made her jump with fright,
The hair belonged to a girl whose face had just gone white.

Lucy climbed up on the ledge, releasing the braid of hair,
And as Rapunzel pulled it back, Lucy stood and stared.
Her regal face was pompous and grim, pretty if she just smiled.
A virtuous maiden she clearly was not, for she was big with child!

Glaring back, Rapunzel scowled
  and hid her bump behind a shawl.
"What are you staring at,
  you ugly thing? I should have let you fall!"
"Welcome milady," Rapunzel sneered,
  her voice rich with disdain,
"I take it you've met my so-called hero,
  a failure, for here I remain."

Ignoring Rapunzel's scornful words, Lucy looked at the room,
A pigsty, cluttered well with combs; the floor in need of a broom.
The door was locked, with one small hatch used for food in the day,
She had to free this awful girl, and then be on her way!

"From all the way up here," she said, "you must see it all."
"Have you seen my sister Ellie, a girl about this tall?"
With her hand up to her chest, she asked with hopeful eyes,
But with the muted blank response, her hope, it swiftly died.

Lucy bit her lip in thought, her eyes upon the hair,
She knew a way to set them free, but could she really dare?
Pulling out her dagger, she beckoned the princess near,
Rapunzel dropped her hair in horror, her eyes wide with fear.

"Murder! Murder!" she cried in terror, falling to her knees:
"For goodness sake!" Lucy said, "enough of that if you please!"
"I need some rope to climb back down; we'll have to use your hair,
Unless of course you have the key – I'd rather use the stairs!"

"It'll grow back," Lucy said, impatiently shaking her head,
"You shouldn't be so vain, would you rather I left you dead?"
Rapunzel stroked her plait of hair, and gave a pitiful moan,
"My beautiful hair!" she whined, and stared at the dagger of bone.

Rapunzel pouted and then let go, "Just do it quick," she said,
Lucy grabbed the golden locks, the knife above her head.
Bringing it down in one swift move and cutting through with ease,
Rapunzel sobbed and clutched her hair, cowering on her knees.

Pulling the bed to the window, she tied the hair to it, tight,
She piled the hair upon the ledge, then pushed with all her might.
Again the braid was flung outside, hitting the floor at last,
Lucy tugged and pulled at the hair, ensuring it held fast.

"I can't climb down!" Rapunzel wailed, "I'm far too scared to try!
I beg you do not make me go, it's simply far too high!"
Lucy sighed and stamped her foot then grabbed the woman's hand,
She had to free Rapunzel if she was to leave this land.

Though fully grown and big with child, Rapunzel's frame was slight,
Lucy could just take her weight, if she held on good and tight.
Rapunzel clung upon her back as Lucy gripped the hair,
Then grit her teeth for both their weight was far too much to bear.

The sky above, now murky pink, had long since lost its glow.
Down they climbed 'til the trees were visible down below.
Again they saw the sobbing prince nestled by his tree,
When he heard them climbing down he fell upon his knees.

And when he heard them touch the ground more salty tears he cried,
"Oh my beloved, she's set you free and brought you to my side!
We'll be together now," he sobbed, "don't fret my precious one,
So long I've waited, sweetest love, for you and my own son!"

He staggered towards with open arms and puckered up his lips,
The princess dodged his warm embrace, her hands upon her hips.
"Foolish boy are you still here? I've told you many a time,
Give up this play for my fair hand: for you, I'm far too fine!"

"Plain you were and plainer still, for now without your eyes,
A brainless twit and foolish too, for you believed my lies!
Leave me now you wretched boy, and bother me no more,
You are not fit to say my name: this child is just not yours!"

How he howled this feeble Prince, clutching at her skirts,
Holding tight as she walked on, his breeches streaked with dirt.
"You do not mean these things you say," he cried in disbelief,
"You wouldn't be so cruel" he sobbed, "to laugh at my own grief?"

Rapunzel walked away from Lucy, dragging the prince along,
The sobbing wretch held on tight, where had he gone wrong?
More concerned was she, it seemed, with her plait of hair,
Which she cradled in her arms, fixed with True Love's stare.

As the wretched pair moved on, Lucy, how she fumed!
Even just a word of thanks she really had assumed.
"I guess you're welcome!" Lucy called, but getting no reply,
On she walked upon the path, under the changing sky.

She'd been too late to save the life
of Little Red Riding Hood

The path beneath grew icy cold and under her feet did crack,
The flowers below the straining glass were wilting into black.
No more bubbles fell from the sky to ping upon her face,
Night was falling, the sky now black and fringed with silver lace.

Lucy tried her best to keep her thoughts from turning sour,
But worse she felt, despair renewed, with every passing hour.
She had not passed her sister yet, they really should be home,
And Ellie must be so afraid, lost and all alone.

It made her sick to think of Ellie, how far could she go?
Her baby sister, was she safe? Lucy had to know!
The peacock trees, no longer bright but twisted, bent and bare,
Their branches grabbed at Lucy's clothes,
    and tangled in her hair.

Lucy cried and freed herself then broke into a run,
As fairies flew above her head, quick to have their fun.
With thorns they poked, bit her skin and pulled her hair with spite,
They cruelly laughed when Lucy tripped and cried out loud in fright.

Lucy felt the tears well up; her knees they throbbed in pain,
With one deep breath, up she stood upon her feet again.
As the fairies laughed and jeered, overcome with glee,
Lucy saw, through her tears, something by a tree.

To the tree she quickly walked, and used her foot to poke,
And soon she saw, indeed it was, a bright red hooded cloak.
Once so pretty, worn with pride, now torn and stained with blood,
Lucy gasped and stumbled back, the cloak left in the mud.

A wave of fear washed over her, panic filled her head;
For Ellie's coat, the one she wore was of the brightest red.
But with a sigh of sick relief, Lucy now recalled:
The coat was left beside the rabbit hole in which she'd crawled.

From in-between the trees, there came a deep and evil sound,
The trees around her shook with roots that trembled in the ground.
Shining through the trees she saw, like diamonds stuck in coal,
A pair of eyes stared back at Lucy, empty with no soul.

The fairies above screamed in fear and scattered through the sky,
Lucy froze, she could not move, too scared to even try.
The pair of eyes grew big in size, surrounded by fur so coarse,
Out it came on four massive paws, a wolf the size of a horse!

Creeping closer he came towards her, eyes locked on his kill,
Lucy tensed and held her breath, being sure to keep so still.
With pointed teeth he snarled, and cocked his massive head,
Between his teeth were scraps of cloth: cloth of the deepest red.

Lucy moaned, her knees went weak, trembling where she stood,
She'd been too late to save the life of Little Red Riding Hood.
What hope had she to beat the wolf, for only small was she,
With just a dagger in her hand, and far too slow to flee.

The wolf dropped his giant head and ran towards his prey,
Lucy screamed and dropped her knife, jumping out the way.
The wolf swung round with such a force, into a tree he crashed,
The dagger on the forest floor, into his paw it slashed.

So great a blow he gave the tree it shifted where it stood,
Giant cracks weaved their way, splitting through the wood.
With fearsome eyes he snarled at Lucy, one paw raised in pain.
He raised his head, howled with rage and shook his silver mane.

He whimpered as he dropped his paw but still he'd not give in,
With graceful steps he circled round, certain he would win.
Lucy matched his every step within this deadly dance,
Standing where she stood before, he took his second chance.

The wolf lowered his giant head, drool hanging from his lips,
His massive tail waved above him, swaying with his hips.
Crouching lower he licked his teeth, ready to attack,
As Lucy felt the damaged tree pressed tight against her back.

He pounced again, paws outstretched, baring his sharp teeth,
Still she stayed, with shaking hands; the ground swaying beneath.
As he lunged she threw herself down upon the ground,
He hit the tree so hard it cracked under the monstrous hound.

This second blow had proved too much, the tree it broke in two,
Its top half fell with deadly force, towards the wolf it flew.
Its branches clawed the open air, the wolf he moved too slow,
Upon his head the tree smashed down and gave its fatal blow.

With a howl the giant wolf crashed down on the floor,
His fearsome eyes like burning coal; he'd open them no more.
Lucy lay there, shaking still, tears rolled down her face,
She closed her eyes and felt her heart beat at such a pace!

Standing up she found the path, and fetched her sharpened bone.
She'd come this far to find her sister; soon they would be home.
Ellie can't have seen the beast; she must have gotten through,
And as the older sister, Lucy knew what she must do.

Two tales she had passed upon her way, now only one remained,
Follow breadcrumbs, burn a witch or fight a dragon chained:
But she cared not, poor tired Lucy, further on she walked,
Til the path of breaking glass came to where it forked.

The path to the left went through the woods, into the dark it weaved,
The path to the right led up a hill; a sight she could not believe.
Upon the hill there stood a castle with rickety towers so tall,
They creaked and groaned, swayed in the wind, almost ready to fall.

Empty it seemed though one light burned, shining from the tower.

Lucy shivered and bent her head as rain came down in showers.

The silver rain it burned her skin and soaked poor Lucy through,

But on she walked towards the tower, the only thing to do.

Ellie must have seen this light; in fact, she could be there!

Being fed by some old woman, giving shelter and care.

Lucy felt such sweet relief, her hope returned once more,

On with newfound strength she walked towards the castle door.

With lips as red as living blood

The path was cracked beyond repair, not fit to walk upon,
So Lucy trudged on through the mud, the sticky grass now gone.
Around her all was dying, no color did remain,
Dark and dismal seemed the world, and on them laid the blame.

Up the hill climbed tired Lucy, soaked right to the skin,
She made her way through wild gardens, unpleasant to be in.
Bushes carved with scary figures, such a creepy sight!
Chilling scenes with trolls and ogres locked in brutal fights.

Through the garden Lucy walked, her feet now thick with mud,
Upon the giant door she knocked, a great resounding thud.
The door it shook and opened with no lock to hold it closed,
So in she went and at the smell her hand flew to her nose.

The dripping rain formed silver puddles on the wooden floor,
The stale air was hard to bear; it made her eyes feel sore.
She stood in a deserted hall, abandoned, layered with dust,
A home to spiders, rats and mice; furniture riddled with rust.

Lucy moved then from the door, walking to the stairs,
"There must be someone here," she thought, "I saw a light up there."
Up the stairs she slowly climbed, and held the rail so tight.
The creaking steps beneath her moved although she was so slight.

At the top a Grandfather clock, long since past its prime,
Its rusty face and twisted hands forever gave false time.
Two archways stood on either side, which led to steps of stone,
Winding way up to the tower, up to someone's home.

Lucy picked which stairs to climb and made her slow ascent,
The tower creaked, unsteady, old, and to the side it leant.
As she climbed it gently swayed and showered down thick dust,
The stones shifted in the wall, stained with damp and rust.

To the very top she climbed, and reached a wooden door,
Light spilt out through gaping cracks and splashed upon the floor.
She knocked and waited for a voice to ask her to come through,
Then pushed her way into the room as her impatience grew.

A beautiful room behind the door, the chambers of a Queen,
A giant bed engraved with leaves, silk sheets of red and cream.
Tapestries hung upon the wall depicting Queens of old,
Windows lined with silken curtains, made of pure spun gold.

Across the room there stood a girl, her hair tangled and wet,
Who jumped in shock and cried with fright, as their wide eyes met.
Her heart beating fast, Lucy laughed, "Look, that girl is me!
A scruffy child with dirty clothes all wet with grubby knees."

Before her stood a looking glass, so elegant and grand,
A wooden frame, layered with gold and roses carved by hand.
Upon a wardrobe the mirror hung, fixed upon the door,
Like tree's roots the wooden base grew right out of the floor.

Within the wardrobe came the sound of someone's muffled cries,
So Lucy reached towards the door as hope flashed in her eyes.
When suddenly behind her came a blaze of purest light,
Then there she stood, a lovely Queen, serenely dressed in white.

In the mirror Lucy stared, she could not look away,
Such a woman she had not seen in all her youthful days.
A beautiful woman, unbearably so, so radiant with light,
With lips as red as living blood and hair as black as night.

The beauty's lips curved in a smile, her black eyes burning bright,
Lucy turned to face her then said out loud "Snow White?"
As she looked upon her face, no longer through the glass,
How she screamed in horror, as the woman cruelly laughed.

A weathered faced, aged through time, skin so dry and stretched,
She had not seen an uglier being than this disgusting wretch!
With bony hands, nails like claws, a blotched and balding head,
Eyes still burning black like coal, but creased and rimmed with red.

"Who are you?" Lucy cried, the glass against her back,
The woman laughed with putrid breath, her teeth decaying, black.
"You were right," she soon replied, her lips curled in a sneer,
Then raised her bony claw-like finger, "Look again my dear."

Lucy turned to face the mirror, shocked at what she saw:
With pale skin and pure white teeth, the beauty stood once more.
"Snow White's gone, my little girl," the red lips said with glee,
"Against her will, her youth and beauty now belong to me."

"That wretched girl, so spoilt was she, chasing flattery so,
So undeserving of her looks, in truth she had to go!
Why should I grow old and ugly, more rotten by the day?
While that brat grew lovelier still, in each and every way?"

"I stole her youth and beauty, now forever will I be
The fairest of them all, I'm told, there's none as fine as me."
Lucy knew not what to say for in the glass it seemed,
She was the fairest of them all and not a festering Queen!

"Who's in there?" she asked instead.

   "There's someone locked inside!"

"Nothing to concern you dear," the Evil Queen replied.

"My sister Ellie!" Lucy cried, "she came here as I'd thought.

Let her go!" she cried out loud, growing quite distraught.

Turning round she gripped the knob and pulled with all her might,

The Evil Queen screamed with rage, her red lips turned to white.

Lucy gasped as she was grabbed and thrown across the floor.

Her body crashed, with a thud, against a chest of drawers.

"Lucy?" came a muffled cry from out behind the door.

"Ellie?" Lucy shouted back, her knees all red and sore.

The wicked Queen, she laughed with spite; "Leave her be!" she said.

"Silly girl, it's your turn first. It's time that I was fed."

"Oh my dear, do you not see the damage you have done?
Just to think that two small girls could drown that shining sun!
Soon the land will swarm with beasts, my creatures of the night,
And swamp the sky with endless black;
    the monsters taking flight."

"As their Queen I'll rule this land, and all will bow to me,
Greatest power is in my hands, my immortality.
Thanks to you, my darling child and the little one,
This world will now belong to me; you see that I have won!"

"Now my dear, come to me – your timing is just right,
Two more girls are all I need to help me with my plight.
Do not fight, I'll make it quick, you'll hardly feel a thing,
I can almost smell your heart, the youth that it will bring!"

With bony hands she beckoned Lucy, black eyes turning white,
Lucy felt her body move, though fought with all her might.
Dark magic swirled around her, a mist of purple smoke,
It filled her eyes, nose and lungs, it made her start to choke.

When close enough to smell her breath, Lucy took her chance,
With all her might she kicked the Queen,
    which freed her from the trance.
The old Queen screamed, a dreadful sound, like banshees in dismay,
"Come back here!" she yelled with rage, "For this I'll make you pay!"

Lucy ran to face the mirror; the beauty glared right back,
Her arms outstretched, racked with rage, eyes returned to black.
Glancing at her gilded mirror, "Don't you dare!" she screamed,
Lucy took her dagger out and in the light it gleamed.

Lucy raised the dagger up, and with a mighty yell,
Drove it through the glass to break the witch's spell.
The mirror cracked as tiny threads wove outwards from the blade,
Like the finest silken web a spider could have made.

Grabbing Lucy by the arm, she threw her to the floor,
The Queen then grabbed the mirror, as it fell from the door;
She looked upon herself, oh how she screamed and wailed,
As the broken mirror groaned and dropped its magic veil.

Her flawless face grew lined and grey; her lips turned white and thin,
Black eyes turned to swampy green; warts grew on her chin.
Reaching out she gripped the dagger with her claw-like hand,
On bended knees
   that creaked and groaned she tried her best to stand.

With a cry she pulled it out, the mirror bent and strained,
It burst into a thousand shards, like silver glassy rain.
Behind the glass, in tattered clothes, there crouched a little girl,
With tear-stained cheeks and dirty hair, a mess of tangled curls.

The Queen defeated, on the floor, engulfed in purple smoke,
It wafted up around her, just like a foggy cloak.
As it slowly disappeared with her stifled moans,
Upon the floor, in one great pile lay the Witch Queen's bones.

Lucy hopped across the bones and to her sister's side,
"Let's go home" she softly said, "We'll skip my turn to hide!"
Ellie wiped her grubby face and took her sister's hand,
"I knew you'd come, please take me home,
    I do not like this land!"

"Little fool," Lucy said, "I thought you would be pleased?"
"Grew tired of wolves and queens, or magic spells?" she teased.
Ellie shook her head and groaned, "It was all so mean:
Crying men, a crazy witch, the biggest wolf I've seen!"

"Come now," Lucy said to her, "we have to hurry back.
We're not welcome in this world; it's fading all to black!"
The sisters left the witch's tower and made their way outside,
But when they saw the once-bright world,
      their shock was hard to hide!

The silver rain had turned to snow and in a blizzard fell,
It turned to ice upon the path, all beauty now dispelled.
Wild winds slashed bare the trees and lightning tore the skies.
It struck the ground and scorched the earth,
      left gaping holes so wide.

Lucy squeezed Ellie's hand; she knew not what to do,
They had to find the way back home;
    they had to journey through.
She'd been told they had to jump from this dying land,
But where to jump once Ellie found, poor Lucy had not planned!

Barren land before them lay, covered in thick snow.
The wind it tore their skin and clothes, pushed them to and fro.
Holding Ellie tight to her, Lucy grit her teeth,
On they walked, their heads bent down, snow lay cold beneath.

Lucy tried hard not to cry, about to give up hope,
When their feet gave way beneath them, upon an icy slope.
Ellie's hand gripped in her own, Lucy held on tight.
All around them tumbled snow, so cold and icy white.

With one free hand Lucy reached for something good to hold,
Soon she found a thick tree root, frozen from the cold.
She grabbed the root and held on tight, lying there quite still,
Her sister's hand still tight in hers, upon the icy hill.

Lucy sat up in the snow, her heart was pounding fast,
Pulling Ellie up beside her, "You ok?" she asked.
Ellie smiled and clapped her hands, "Again!" she said with glee,
Lucy frowned and looked around, knelt upon her knees.

A deep abyss of swirling smoke, a chasm in the ground,
Lucy knew without a doubt the land's edge had been found.
"We have to jump!" Lucy cried, the winds around her howled,
"I don't want to!" Ellie said; her face creased in a scowl.

Overhead she heard the screams of monsters taking flight,
The ground beneath began to shake with creatures of the night,
That burrowed up from where they slept
    to make their presence known,
To wreak their havoc on this world and make the land their own.

Lucy knew she had no choice; they had to face their fears,
She closed her eyes, gripped Ellie's hand,
    held back her frightened tears.
As the ground beneath her shook and threatened to give way,
Lucy ran and made her jump, into the swirling grey.

What a dream to have!

With a jolt Lucy woke, lying on her bed,
Surrounded by her stuck-on stars shining overhead.
In silent shock she looked around, though did not trust her eyes,
For in her room was she, it seemed, much to her surprise.

Here she was, safe and sound, tucked up in her bed,
Could it all have been imagined – played out in her head?
The strangest dream she'd ever had, and scary it was too,
Could it all have really happened, could it all be true?

"Ellie!" Lucy said aloud, her sister was she here?
Again she felt that panic rise, that cold and numbing fear.
But to her left Ellie slept, tucked up in her bed,
Snoring slightly in content, the blankets round her head.

Snuggling down into her bed she gave a little sigh,

"What a dream to have!" she thought, in which she'd nearly died!

Twisted tales, giant monsters, burning silver rain,

Girls with wings and evil witches out to cause you pain.

Lucy pulled her covers up,
    but found them wet and cold,
So threw them off, and such a sight,
    she did now behold!
Her feet were filthy, caked in mud,
    with cuts upon the toes,
With matted hair, bruised sore hands,
    and dressed in soggy clothes.

"It can't be real!" she said aloud,
    "It must have been a dream.
All those things I thought I'd done
    and all that I have seen!"
Then in her pocket something moved
    and stabbed her in the thigh,
She turned her fraying pockets out
    and gave a startled cry.

On her hand there sat a fairy, with a tiny thorn,
Grumpy-faced with crumpled wings, her pretty dress all torn.
"Were you with me for all this time?" she asked of her new friend,
"You bit my nose you little cur! Are you here to make amends?"

The fairy flew out of her hand then swiftly turning round,
It made a face, shook its fist and spat upon the ground.
It hovered closer with a smile, all elegance and grace,
Then mightily, it threw the thorn, which bounced off Lucy's face.

Lucy was just lost for words but in her head she heard,
Zephyr's voice, so sweet and light, it sang those truthful words:
"Never trust a fairy's tale, for fairies just tell lies...
And never cross a fairy if you value both your eyes!"

The End

About the Author

Rachael Fuller grew up in West Somerset, UK, where she spent her teenage years acting, singing, writing poems and daydreaming of fair maidens and knights in shining armor. Looking to the Brothers Grimm for inspiration, Rachael spurs her vivid imagination by sharing her stories and rhyme with anyone who understands the need for good old-fashioned story-telling, not just children but also adults who long for more than just the reality they live in everyday.

She currently lives in St. Albans with her fiancé Carl Stuart-MacRae.

You can visit her webpage at www.rachaelfuller.co.uk/faerytale/

Lightning Source UK Ltd.
Milton Keynes UK
UKOW052144041111

181415UK00001BA/1/P